Everybody
Say Cheese

OTHER YEARLING BOOKS YOU WILL ENJOY:

YEARLING BOOKS are designed especially to entertain and enlighten young people. Charles F. Reasoner, Professor Emeritus of Children's Literature and Reading, New York University, is consultant to this series.

For a complete listing of all Yearling titles, write to
Dell Publishing Co., Inc., Promotion Department,
P.O. Box 3000, Pine Brook, N.J. 07058.

Everybody Say Cheese

Betty Bates

Illustrated by Jim Spence

A YEARLING BOOK

Published by
Dell Publishing Co., Inc.
1 Dag Hammarskjold Plaza
New York, New York 10017

This work was first published under the title of *Say Cheese*.

Yearling ® TM 913705, Dell Publishing Co., Inc.

ISBN: 0-440-42446-1

Reprinted by arrangement with Holiday House

Printed in the United States of America

October 1986

10 9 8 7 6 5 4 3 2 1

CW

For two of my favorite readers
BETHANY *and* CHRIS

Contents

Everybody
Say Cheese

1.

Dang Blast It!

If my dad didn't have the habit of singing at his work-bench, there wouldn't have been all that crazy business about the hundred-dollar check. He's got a voice like a truck dumping gravel, and he blasts out "Some Enchanted Evening" and "Mack, the Knife" and "Raindrops Keep Fallin' on My Head." All the nutty old songs from movies and musicals and way back when. He sings just about everything except songs in foreign languages, because Mom says he gets the pronunciation wrong.

So on the Saturday after Thanksgiving, I was minding my own business, doing my housework for the week, part of which is taking care of weekend lunches for the seven of us. I've got a flock of brothers and

3

sisters, two of each. Then there are Mom and Dad. Everyone wonders how they can afford three girls and two boys on what Dad makes as a mechanic and what Mom makes from selling her quilts, and from her wedding-and-funeral flower service. One secret is that we kids earn every penny we can, and the other secret is that the family does everything for itself that it can. Dad's got his workroom, and Mom knits and sews most of our clothes, and in the fall we all get busy and put up tomatoes and beans from the garden, even Mims, the youngest.

So there I was, setting those seven places, snapping my gum and chug-chugging around the kitchen table to the rhythm of the music on the radio. All of a sudden Fuzz Fuller, the disk jockey, cut in. "Hey hey, all you listeners out there, it's time for our name-that-song contest. Listen carefully while we play the first few bars of a song, because if you know what it is, you could win our hundred-dollar jackpot. Yes, one hundred dollars, folks."

All the things I could do with that money flashed through my mind. I could invest in a stereo, or get my own private TV set, or buy some really zowie outfit to impress Gilbert Trowbridge in my fifth-grade church school class.

"Now," said Fuzz Fuller, "the first person who calls 222–WHAM with the correct name of the song will be the lucky winner. Are you ready?"

The tune came on, and you could have knocked me over with a toothpick. It was "Kitty McQuitty," one of Dad's favorites. I raced for the kitchen phone and dialed the number. I was sure I'd get the busy signal. There must be thousands of adults calling in, people who remember the old songs.

Somebody answered. "Station WHAM. Gwen speaking."

"'Kitty McQuitty,'" I screamed, accidentally spitting out my gum. I don't know why I screamed, but it seemed like the thing to do.

Gwen giggled. "'Kitty McQuitty' is right. Now I want to get your name and address, and you'll be talking with Fuzz."

I scooped my gum off the floor and shoved it back into my mouth. "You mean I'm the first?" I've never been first at anything. With my brothers and sisters I'm in the middle. Always third, whether we start with the youngest or the oldest.

"Your name, please." Gwen's voice was now very crisp and no-nonsense, like Mom's when she's getting dinner, sterilizing jars, and having to go to the bathroom, all at the same time.

"My name's Christine Hooper. Only I get called Christy."

"And your address?"

"Forty-seven sixteen Carmichael Street."

"Thank you, Christy. Here's Fuzz."

Fuzz! I felt as if my bones had completely disappeared. What should I say to Fuzz Fuller, the well-known disk jockey?

"Hello there, Christy."

"Mm—hello." There was something stuck in my throat. A large sock, maybe.

"Are you there, Christy?"

I cleared my throat. "I'm here," I said faintly, as if I was talking through the back of my neck.

"Say, Christy, are you willing to tell your age? Remember we've got millions of people listening, heh heh."

"I'm ten. Ten and one-third."

"Ten and a third. So tell me how you knew the name of that song. It's an old song, Christy, and you're young."

Young! Ten and a third isn't all that young.

"Well, see, my dad sings it. He's got a workroom, and he's making a new piece for Mom's quilting frame because it accidentally got jumped on by my younger brother Damon, and he's been down in the basement a lot singing. He knows all the old songs, and he tosses in lots of slides and trills."

"Hm. Maybe he could cut a record. How's his voice?"

"Um, well—"

"Never mind. Do you know the words to 'Kitty McQuitty,' Christy?"

"Sure. I've heard them a million times."

"A million times in ten years?"

"Ten and a third."

"Right. Then I'll bet you could sing them for me, huh?"

"Me? Sing?"

"Sure. Bet you could do at least as well as your dad. Come on, Christy, let's have it. Mi-mi-mi."

So I nudged my gum into my cheek and sang:

> Kitty McQuitty is pretty.
> Kitty is my honeybee.
> I'll stick to my Kitty McQuitty
> Till my honey quits sticking
>   to me.

"Terrific!" said Fuzz. "You've got a great pair of tonsils, Christy."

"Thanks." I was feeling pretty good. I'd remembered the words, and I hadn't burped in the middle.

"You'll get that check in the mail on Monday, Christy. And thanks for listening to WHAM."

He hung up. My moment of fame was past, and nobody in my family had heard me. We live on top of each other in a little old two-story gray frame house with dark green shutters. Usually it's a monkey house, with doors slamming, my thirteen-year-old sister Ursula monopolizing some phone conversation, and what Mom calls lively discussions and I call fights. But now, except for the Fuzz Fuller program, and except for Dad's voice seeping through the register singing "Bill Bailey," accompanied by the hum of his power saw, there was silence.

The singing stopped. "Blast! It's busted!" It was Dad's voice from the basement. There was the heavy clump-clump of his feet on the stairs, and he showed up in the kitchen.

He had his power saw in those thick hands of his, and he looked as if he'd swallowed an entire onion. "It's burned out," he said, slamming the basement door behind him. Only it didn't slam because the cord hanging down from the saw was in the way. "Dang blast it!" My dad doesn't believe in swearing, but sometimes he comes one thin line away from it. He yanked the cord up and wrapped it around the saw, muttering.

"And now," Fuzz Fuller was saying, "the song that's drenching the country, 'Your Eyes Are Like Two Umbrellas.'"

I snapped the radio off. Somehow the song didn't seem to fit. "Say, Dad, did you hear me singing?"

"Singing? You singing?"

"See, I recognized 'Kitty McQuitty.'"

He was frowning at the saw. "I'll have to get a new

one when I get the money together. What did you say about recognizing some girl?"

"Dad, you know the song. It was on WHAM, and I called in and won a hundred dollars."

I had his attention.

"You won a hundred dollars?"

"Right."

"Well now, Christy, I never knew you could sing that well."

"That's not the idea. See, it's—oh, forget it."

"You slam that money into your savings account the minute the check comes." He nodded his head very firmly, opened the back door, and took off toward the garage.

When Dad nods his head that way, he means business.

2.

I'm Always Getting Interrupted

At lunchtime my kid brother Damon brought Mims in from the backyard. Since she's only four, he had to help her peel off her jacket. I could hear my big brother Ben charging down the stairs three at a time, rattling windows.

Mom carried in one of her flower arrangements for the Trowbridge wedding that evening. While she was setting it in the middle of the kitchen table, Dad stomped in from the garage. Mom examined her bouquet from every angle, rubbing her chin thoughtfully. It looked gorgeous, like spun gold.

Finally Ursula drifted into the kitchen with her hair pulled back and tied in a scarf. "Buenos días, everybody." She'd been dumping her junior high Spanish on us all year. She's obviously got a crush on Mr. Sharp, her Spanish teacher, whom she calls El Sharpo.

"Great flower arrangement, Mom," said Ben.

"Thanks, honey. I could have used more mums to make it fuller, but it will have to do."

Mom says a flower arrangement is a mirror of the soul. She usually tries her bouquets out on us during meals. That way she gets double use out of them.

I was at the stove dishing out the homemade soup Mom had made from the day-before-yesterday's Thanksgiving turkey. It had pieces of stuff in it. Beans and carrots and celery and onions, like some messed-up liquid garden. Mom says all those things are good for the digestion. What I want to know is, how does she know? I don't like extra things in my soup. Turkey soup should be just plain turkey soup.

But this time I didn't especially care, because I was full of my news. "Guess what, everybody. I won—"

"Christy dear," said Mom, "get that gum out of your mouth and make it fast."

By this time the gum was ancient anyway. As I sat down, I slipped it out of my mouth and stuck it to the bottom of my chair, making sure no one was looking.

Mims was giving us that smile of hers that wraps itself around your heart, or your gizzard, or whatever. "Damon and I made leaf mountains."

"Right," said Damon. "I raked the leaves into mountains, and you jumped in and messed them up."

"Sure I did. It's fun."

"Sisters stink." Damon was still missing a front tooth, so what he said sounded like "Thithters thtink."

"Damon," said Dad, "cut out the nasty talk."

"Hey, everybody," I said, "listen."

"Mom," said Ursula, "after lunch could you give me a perm? My hair looks awful." Her hair looked a little stringy maybe, around that face of hers that's small and delicate, like some pixie's. Her hair is mud-colored like her eyes, but it's okay.

"Honey," said Mom, "I'll be busy taking the flowers over to the church. Remember, the wedding's at five o'clock."

"Hey, you guys, Fuzz Fuller's sending me—"

"Can't you get Ben to take the flowers?" wailed Ursula.

"Me?" said Ben. "I've got to get my camera and film ready. I'm the official wedding photographer, remember?"

"Listen, everybody—"

"Power saw's busted," said Dad.

"Busted?" asked Ben.

"Motor burned out."

"Hey, you guys, I'm trying to tell you—"

"That's awful," said Damon. "Now you can't fix the quilting frame."

"And how am I supposed to finish my quilt?" asked Mom.

This was trouble. Power saws must cost millions.

"You shouldn't have busted that frame, Damon," said Ben.

"Well, how was I supposed to know Mims had accidentally knocked it over?"

"You shouldn't go jumping off of beds."

"Mom, can't you please give me that perm? I need—"

"Now listen, everybody. Will you kindly listen to me?"

"Christy," said Mom, "you mustn't interrupt."

"I did not interrupt. You were all interrupting me. You wouldn't let me say one thing."

There was silence.

Finally Mom said, "I guess you're right, honey, now that I think about it."

"I'm always getting interrupted. Every time I open my mouth and start to say something, somebody cuts me off."

"Just raise your hand," said Damon, "the way we do at school." He always wants to do everything the way they do it in third grade.

So why not go along? I raised my hand. "I won a hundred dollars."

"Christy," said Mom, "please stick to the truth. The

truth can't ever hurt you."

"I know that, Mom, but—"

"It's true," said Dad. "She won some singing contest on the radio."

"It was not a singing contest. It was a name-that-song contest, and I'm getting the check on Monday, so there."

Ben quit slurping his soup. Ursula, who was taking a bite out of a cracker, shut her mouth. Damon upset his spoon, spilling dabs of vegetables all over the place. Mims rested her chin on the edge of the table and stared. And Mom's eyebrows came together in one thin, sandy line.

I didn't mind having all the attention. Maybe I could win the next WHAM contest, and the next, and the next. By the time I got through winning, I'd have enough money to sail to Europe on the *Queen Elizabeth II*. I once saw an ad that said the food on that ship is real gourmet stuff, and I could come back and tell Gilbert Trowbridge all about it. Anyway, I'll bet they don't have anything as dull as turkey soup with vegetables.

Ben set his spoon down and threw back his big shoulders. "Hey, Christy-Wisty, old pal, Christmas is coming. How about—"

"Now you listen, Ben Hooper," said Mom, "it's Christy's money. I won't have anybody telling her what to do with it, you hear?" Mom's a redhead, like me, and when she gets into a boil she shakes her head so her curls spill over her forehead.

"Right," said Dad. "I don't want anybody bugging Christy about that check. It's hers. Of course, I think it ought to go straight to the bank. You'll need all the money you can get for college, Christy."

I don't want to go to college. Ursula does, and Ben does, but I don't. I want to marry Gilbert and work in a chewing gum plant.

Ursula was watching me from across the table, blinking those brown eyes of hers. Did she have plans for my money too? Now that she's in eighth grade, it seems as if she always needs money for a new blouse or a home perm. And Ben was still giving me the eye. Damon was looking at me sideways. Even Mims was staring, and sucking her finger.

In our family we mostly trade small, homemade gifts for Christmas. But this time everyone would probably expect diamonds and rubies.

It was like being trapped in some revolving door.

3.

What Ben Wanted

Gilbert's big sister Elissa was marrying a policeman
built like a gorilla. Gilbert, with his ears like sugar-
bowl handles, was an usher in a bow tie and one of
those frilly shirts. He galloped me down the church
aisle in about five seconds and all but shoved me into
the pew as if I had some very tropical disease. Maybe
it was the dress I had on. It was rose-colored, with
puffs at the tops of the long sleeves. Mom had made
it for Ursula to wear to Ben's graduation from junior
high two and a half years ago. Mom calls it *empire*,
pronouncing it the French way, awm-peer. I call it
yuck.

Rose may be Ursula's color, but it's not mine. It

looks awful with my red hair. Besides, the dress was way too short for me. Mom says I'm getting my growth extra early. This is all very well when we play volleyball at school, where the other girls want to be on the same team with me and my extra height, but it has definite disadvantages.

While we were sitting lined up in the pew with the organ playing softly, I kept itching to pull the skirt down, except it wouldn't have pulled down.

I must have looked like somebody's bad dream.

I wished Mom would make me a new dress. She never has time. I always have to wait for Ursula to outgrow hers, and now, of course, the yellow one Ursula had on was exactly right for her. You didn't see her twitching in the pew as if she'd give bags of bubble gum to be able to tug her skirt down.

Just wait till I got that check. I'd get myself a new dress for sure.

When I was sure Mom wasn't looking, I popped a piece of gum into my mouth and chewed hard.

Mom's altar bouquets looked sensational, all yellow roses and mums. It didn't seem to matter that there weren't enough mums. Anyway, Mom's never satisfied when she makes things. And she always cries at weddings. She cried at this one, especially when Marva York, the soloist who's the teller at the bank, sang "To

Each His Own" while rolling her handkerchief into a ball.

Afterward, at the reception in the church house, Ben went around snapping pictures, perspiring like a drippy faucet. He took one of Gilbert's sister Elissa, with her veil slightly crooked, and the gorilla, beaming at each other. Then Elissa and her bridesmaids in their filmy blue gowns. And then the gorilla, Gilbert, and the other males in the wedding lined up as if they were ready to break into a song.

Gilbert is short and skinny like a straw, with a lock of hair near the back of his head that points toward the ceiling. The fact that he's shorter than I am is no surprise, since nearly every boy in my class is shorter than nearly every girl. But he's got deep blue eyes and a very appealing dent in his chin. Of course, if he knew I was thinking those things, he'd advise me to take my temperature.

After the picture-snapping of the wedding party, Ben wiped his face and stopped to change his film. Gilbert shot toward the food-and-punch table, grabbed a couple of those little round hamburgers, and began shoving them down his throat. This was my chance. I was elbowing my way through the crowd when a voice blasted out at me. "Hello there, Christy dear."

It was Dad's sister, Aunt Sadie, looking as if she had on a small tent that was about to split at the seams.

If you're not careful, she's good for a half hour of talking. She gave me a doubtful look, pulling her eyebrows together. "I suppose your mother made that dress."

"Uh huh. She made it for Ursula."

"Well, of course. Now I remember. It looked lovely on Ursula."

Aunt Sadie doesn't mean to be tactless. The words just come out that way. "Didn't Marva York sing well?" she asked. "A little flat, but still it was nice."

"Right, Aunt Sadie. Excuse me, Aunt Sadie, but I, um, have to go."

Luckily Gilbert was still digging into the sandwiches. I tore across the room. "Hello, Gilbert."

He gave me a quick glance, and I caught the flash of those blue eyes. Then he glued them on the punch bowl. "Oh, um, hi, Hooper." He always calls me by my last name. Is that an encouraging sign? Come to think of it, he calls everybody by their last names, and so do the other guys in my class.

"Nice wedding." I reached for a hamburger.

"What're you planning to do with the money?"

"What money?"

He almost looked at me. "I heard you win the contest."

"You did? You were listening to Fuzz Fuller?"

"Right. I heard you sing. Had you just swallowed

something sharp?"

"Gilbert Trowbridge, are you implying that my voice—"

"I'm not implying anything. I was only taking an interest in your vocal cords."

I would have liked to sock him, but you can't sock somebody whose sister has just got married to a gorilla. So I merely stuck my tongue out at him, which naturally he didn't see on account of the way he hardly ever looks at me. "Try to get run over by a bus," I said, and took off. Just because my voice isn't opera-star quality, he thought he could talk to me about swallowing sharp things. I was wounded through and through. Even my fingernails hurt.

I gulped half the hamburger, along with my gum. The whole mess tasted like rubber boots.

When I got back to the corner of the room where my family was, it turned out Ben was ready to send out a search party for me since he was set to take a picture of all the Hoopers. The whole family was standing there like a picture in a comic strip. "So there you are, Christy-Wisty," said Ben.

I wish he wouldn't call me that.

"Where've you been?" asked Dad.

"Oh, just around. Do I have to have my picture taken in this rag?"

Mom gave me a sudden, very thoughtful look, but

Dad said, "Honeybun, you look gorgeous. Of course you've got to be in the picture." He drew me over between himself and Aunt Sadie.

Ben grabbed Gilbert's dad as he passed by and asked him to snap the picture, and then Ben came and stood next to Mom. "Everybody smile now. Say cheese."

I frowned.

After we'd crammed wedding cake down our throats, and after somebody had stuffed rice down the back of Elissa's going-away suit as she and the gorilla took off for their car, it was time for us to leave. Outside, it was snowing. When we were jammed into our beat-up old Plymouth, with Ben's concrete shoulder keeping me in my corner, he said into my ear, "This camera of mine certainly could use a tripod."

"How come it needs a tripod?"

"Tripods are very handy for keeping a camera steady in certain situations. If I had one I could have taken a delayed-action picture of all of us without having to get Mr. Trowbridge to do it. Besides, a tripod would have helped when I took the formal pictures. A photographer who doesn't have one looks unprofessional. He hasn't got any dignity."

I've never known a time when Ben was dignified, so why did he bring up dignity all of a sudden?

Ursula, who was holding Mims on her lap, must have overheard, because she said, "Ben, you aren't supposed to ask Christy for things."

"Who said I was asking? I was only remarking that it's unprofessional not to have a tripod."

"Ben, you know perfectly well what you're doing. You might as well just ask Christy for a tripod for Christmas. Anyway, a tripod's nowhere near as important as an easel."

"An easel? Who said anything about an easel? And besides, who asked you to join our private conversation?"

It happens that Ursula is very artistic and that she turns out terrific water colors and sketches, but this was ridiculous.

"Ben," said Dad from the front seat, "that's enough."

"Golly, Dad, I was only making small talk with Christy, and Ursula had to go and blow it up into a regular town meeting."

"I said, that's enough, Ben."

When we got home, I made for the room I share with Mims. Even though I'm often very fond of Mims, I actually consider the room mine because, after all, I was there first. Besides, I do wish sometimes that it were still all mine, and I envy Ursula, who's the only one in our family with a room to herself. It's awfully hard for me to get any privacy with Mims buzzing in and out.

It's a small room with my single bed and the bed

Dad made to match it when Mims got too big for her crib. There's a window, a bureau with a mirror, and a straight wooden chair Mom inherited from her mother. The bedspreads are cotton, with pictures of different-colored balloons on them. I mean, balloons! I'm too old for that kind of thing.

You can hardly see Mims's bedspread, because it's just about covered with dolls, some of which Mom made for her. Mims is crazy about dolls, and she talks to them all the time, especially Zinnia. Zinnia's missing one button eye, but Mims won't let Mom give her another. Mims seems to have this very urgent need to comfort somebody—or is it something? I mean, is Zinnia a thing or a person?

I flopped onto my bed and picked up the Priscilla Pierce detective book I'd taken out of the town library, *The Missing Teeth Mystery*. I was thinking of the nasty remark Gilbert had made. And Ben. Did he have the idea I was some kind of bank?

Ben does have a tough time, because he's got to buy his equipment and pay his school expenses out of what he makes with his photography and his job at the drugstore after school. So maybe I could find it in my heart to forgive him. But how could I forgive Gilbert for his crack about my singing? Maybe I should make some nasty remark to him at church school tomorrow, like calling him a peanut or telling him I'd like to pull him inside out and make him swallow himself. But that way I'd lose him forever, not that I had him in the first place.

As I opened the book, I found myself sighing. Somehow all the meaning had gone out of my life.

4.

What Damon Wanted

The next morning there was a whole bunch more snow on the ground, so Mom announced we'd all have to wear boots. Mims said she wouldn't, because she hates my old ones, which are too big for her, but Mom said to get those boots on lickety-split and no back talk, so Mims ended up pouting and flopping around as if she were playing dress-up.

In church school I ignored Gilbert completely. I sat on the other side of the room by the windows and tried not to look at him, especially while he was describing to Mr. Waterbury how the prodigal son must have felt when he found himself alone and friendless. I hoped Gilbert felt the same way. Since he's not in my room at school, I didn't get many chances to ignore him there, so I had to make the most of Sundays.

The trouble was that after class he started giggling and playing around with Jeremy Wick, not seeming to notice me ignoring him. He wasn't the least bit alone and friendless. It was enough to make a person feel like some kind of insect.

Out in the hall, Damon popped out of the third-grade classroom juggling walnuts, which I happen to love. "Where'd you get the walnuts, Damon?"

"Miss Cress gave them to us. She says they're symbols of Advent. 'In a wooden, worthless shell lies a hidden sweet kernel, the symbol of life.'"

"Oh, right." My mind wasn't on wooden, worthless shells. It was on the kernel inside, and my mouth was watering. But Damon went right on juggling those nuts.

Back at home, as Dad drove the car into our garage, I noticed the power saw sitting on the shelf, broken and forlorn. Like the prodigal son. And like me.

How come Dad hadn't thrown the saw away? Maybe he expected it to come back to life.

I was on my way to my room to change from my skirt into jeans when I glanced into Dad and Mom's room, where Mom had sat down to baste together Ben's new suit. She was using every spare minute, since the suit he was wearing showed off his wrists and ankles.

On the big hinge-topped chest at the foot of the bed sat the quilt. It was mostly white, and pieced into a star pattern with patches of colored material from old dresses and shirts. I'd spotted bits of the blouse I'd ripped when I climbed the back fence chasing a ball, and the pajamas that got the seat torn when I was getting over chicken pox and slid down the banister.

Mom had drawn lines for the stitching and basted the layers together, and the whole thing was ready to be quilted after Dad got the new saw and made the new part for the frame. It was a special frame that Mom could use in their little bedroom, a lot smaller than the old-fashioned ones.

Mom learned how to make quilts from her mother, on the farm outside of town where she grew up, and she sells them to the Slumber Shop for a whole lot of money. We always seem to need that money for something or other. Only this time she'd positively promised herself that that quilt was going on the big bed that belongs to her and Dad.

Maybe she could have sold it to get money for the saw, only she couldn't because there was no saw to fix the quilting frame.

I guess that's what you call an extremely vicious circle.

When Mom spotted me, she said, "Christy, you will remember to set a place for Aunt Sadie at dinner tonight, won't you?"

"Sure, Mom."

She was giving me one of her thoughtful looks. Was

she remembering how awful I'd looked in that dress last night?

In the room Damon and Ben share, they were talking about how to escape in case of fire. "You can tie sheets together," said Damon. "You can knot one end around the leg of your bed." Since he was juggling scarves instead of the walnuts, I figured he must have eaten the walnuts. Actually he's a pretty good juggler, considering his extreme youth. He puts on shows with scarves that Mom made him, and a few magic tricks, for little kids' birthday parties around town. Dad helped him figure out some pretty good background patter to go along with his act, including a couple of really funny knock-knock jokes. I'd heard that the kids nearly always clapped for more, except that he hadn't worked up an encore yet.

"Sure," said Ben with a yawn. "You could go to the trouble of tying sheets together. But first you might check out the hall and stairs, the way we practiced it."

A scarf bounced off Damon's freckles and fell to the floor. As he scooped it up, he happened to look my way. He pretended he hadn't seen me, but he had. I could tell by the way his ears wiggled. "Know what I want for Christmas, Ben?"

"What?"

"A strongbox."

"Huh?"

"You know. One of those metal things you keep important stuff in. You can lock it so it's private."

"You mean so I can't get at your junk, huh?" Ben gave him a wink.

"Right."

I could see Damon's point. I felt the same way.

Since I was planning to make toasted cheese-lettuce-onion-and-peanut butter sandwiches for lunch, I unplugged the fridge when I got back down to the kitchen. Otherwise I'd blow a fuse when I turned on the toaster oven. Putting in more wiring was on Dad's list of jobs to do around the house, but he hadn't got around to it, and the list seemed to get longer and longer.

At lunch, Dad took a bite of his sandwich, winced, and said, "What have we here?"

"They're very good," said Mom, loyally backing me up.

"Oh. Well, if you say so." Dad took a few quick breaths in and out and turned to Damon. "It's your turn to shovel the sidewalks, Damon."

Damon was gobbling his sandwich. He loves crazy food. He swallowed. "Do I have to shovel the sidewalks? I've got another magic show coming up the day after Christmas, and I've got to practice."

"There's plenty of time. You can do that later."

"I hate shoveling snow."

"Well, if you're too weak and puny—"

"Okay, okay, I'll do it."

All through the meal I kept expecting somebody to mention Christmas gifts. I couldn't get the idea out of my head that everybody was thinking about them in connection with my check. It was like waiting to get called on in school when I haven't read the assignment. But we actually got finished without one person mentioning something that person couldn't live without.

After lunch I brought my book down to the living room so I could read in peace, away from Mims. I was struggling to get Priscilla Pierce sprung out of the back of a locked moving van roaring down the thruway when Damon went out to shovel the front sidewalk, which is about as long as my little finger. He hadn't been outside more than a minute when the front door slammed and he turned up in the front hall. "Hey, Dad."

Dad was up in Ursula's room putting in weather stripping. "I'm upstairs, Damon. Come here if you want to talk to me."

"But I'm full of snow, and the shovel's falling apart."

I could hear Dad's sigh. "All right. I noticed the bolts were loose, but I didn't have time to take care of it. I'll be down, and we'll do it together."

"So you want a strongbox," I said to Damon.

"Did you hear me say that?"

"You know I heard you say that."

"Well, I do. I'd need a lock too."

Now I knew what Santa must feel like.

"Know what, Christy?"

"No. What?"

"I wish I was an only child."

I thought about that. "Sure. But then you wouldn't have us. You wouldn't have Ben or Ursula or Mims or me."

"Right." He was grinning. Grinning. "I wouldn't miss you because I wouldn't know you."

"Damon, that's a terrible thing to say."

"I know. I guess I didn't actually mean it. Know something else I want for Christmas?"

"What?"

"I want my tooth. I want to quit talking funny."

His lip was trembling.

"Damon, you'll get your tooth soon. I know you will."

Just then Dad came downstairs.

Mom always gets our dinners, and till tomorrow, when we'd all switch jobs, it was my job to help her. On Sundays Aunt Sadie's usually with us. Mom says there's always a chair at our table for Aunt Sadie, only I'm afraid that some day it's going to collapse underneath her.

When I thumped into the basement to get a couple of jars of stewed tomatoes, Ben was backing his big body out of the closet he uses as a darkroom, and locking the door. "Hey, Christy, the wedding pictures turned out okay. Want to see?"

"Sure."

I took a look. The one of Elissa and her new husband was fine, except for her crooked veil. The males in the party all looked handsome, even though Gilbert's ears stuck out. The females, in their blue dresses, looked okay. There was the minister and his wife. And there, all of a sudden, were the Hoopers. Us.

I looked awful.

"I look awful, Ben."

"Well, what did you expect when you made a face as if you'd been bitten in the leg?"

"It wouldn't have been hard to bite me in the leg. Just look at how short that dress is. It's indecent."

"Come on, Christy-Wisty, it's not so bad."

"Do me a favor, Ben. Quit calling me Christy-Wisty."

He grinned. "I'll try to remember."

It wasn't any use. He'd never quit.

"Do me another favor?"

"No."

"But you don't even know what it is."

"I do too. You want me to tear up this picture and pretend it didn't come out, the way I did with the one I took of you in the bathing suit."

"That was summer before last, when I was bulging

out of Ursula's old suit like some balloon."

Now I could picture Gilbert's face when he saw that family picture. He'd never ever want to look at me again. "Please, Ben."

"Listen, if I tore it up it wouldn't be fair to the rest of the family. Besides, what do you think people would say about the Hooper Photo Service? They'd say it was rotten. The news would be all over town."

Maybe I could snitch the picture before he delivered it to the Trowbridges. Only now he was putting them all into an envelope and sticking the envelope in his pocket, and the negatives were locked in the darkroom closet.

Why had I done such a dumb thing?

5.

What Mims Wanted

By the time I got up from the basement, the kitchen was warm and spicy smelling. Mom puts all kinds of mysterious stuff on her baked chicken, stuff that seeps into your nose and comforts it.

Ben, following behind me, snitched two of the brownies Mom makes for Sundays and holidays only. When I turned and saw him with one in each hand, I nearly threw the tomatoes at him. "Ben, you cut that out."

He gave me that grin of his that almost touches his ears. "But they're so good. How could I resist?"

"Benjamin Hooper," said Mom, "you're getting too big for your britches. You're not to have any brownies at dinner, you hear?"

38

Ben didn't argue. He knew she meant business.

"Christy," said Mom, "how come the fridge light doesn't turn on and the black walnut ice cream in the freezer section is half melted?"

Crum! I'd forgotten to plug in the fridge after I used the toaster oven at lunchtime. "Oh, Mom!"

"Never mind, honey, we'll serve it anyway."

"Do we have to?"

"Yes, we have to."

Double crum!

After I'd set the table, I went upstairs to fix myself up before dinner. Mims was in the bathroom. I could hear her talking to Zinnia. She always takes Zinnia into the bathroom and pretends to wash her hands and face, and she takes forever. She hasn't figured out yet that when you're a member of a family of seven you need to get in and out fast.

I ducked into the bedroom and combed my hair at the bureau, inspecting myself in the mirror, checking out the seventeen freckles across my nose and cheeks and the way my ears make my curls stick out.

Mims was still in the bathroom.

It was five minutes to six. Aunt Sadie would be coming at six, and I needed to mash the potatoes. Back in the hall, I knocked on the bathroom door. "Mims, I have to get in there."

"How come?"

"Never mind how come."

"Christy, you're mean. Everybody's always mean to me."

"That's not true. We're always very kind to you."

"You're mean because I'm the youngest."

"Mims."

"And because you're bigger than me."

"Mims!"

"Huh?"

"Get out of there."

"I will not."

"I'm going to hide all the rest of your dolls. I'm leaving here right now to get them and put them where you'll never find them, and they'll completely rot away."

"Christy, you stop it!"

The door opened, and there was Mims, holding tight to Zinnia. Her lower lip was sticking out. She marched straight past me into our room.

Before I went downstairs, I poked my head into the bedroom. Mims was lying on her bed glaring at the ceiling. She looked very small and white, like some corpse.

"I'm sorry, Mimsie."

No answer.

I had a pretty good idea how she felt. "It's hard to get any privacy around here, right?"

"Right. It's hard to get any privacy." She pronounced the word prive-see, but I had a feeling she'd figured out what it meant.

At dinner, Aunt Sadie told us about the artist who lives in the apartment down the hall who painted a modern mural on his wall, all red and purple and orange, and had a fight about it with the landlord. "He showed it to me," she said. "You need sunglasses to look at it." She shook her head so her chins jiggled.

Aunt Sadie has a voice like a plane taking off. We always listen to Aunt Sadie. She asked each one of us about our lives. Damon talked about doing his magic and juggling act at a birthday party last weekend, when he missed catching a scarf, which fell into somebody's hot chocolate and got all brown and drippy, so he had to carry on with a sticky scarf. Aunt Sadie gave her bugle-call laugh. "Now who else but you would have been able to do that, Damon sweetie?" While Damon stuck his nose in the air, she turned to me. "All right, Christy, tell me what you're up to."

I told about winning the contest.

"So those songs your dad sings are good for something after all," she boomed.

Ursula told her she had to give a report in Spanish class tomorrow on the agriculture of Spain. "My teacher believes we ought to have the background of the country whose language we're studying."

"Absolutely," said Aunt Sadie.

Mom and I started passing out the dessert. Aunt Sadie ignored her soupy ice cream. "Did the wedding pictures come out, Ben?"

"Yep. They're great. I'll show them to you after dinner."

"Ben Hooper," I yelled, "don't you dare show that picture of us."

"Come on, Christy. Just because you didn't come out looking like some model."

"Can I help it if my dress is too short?"

"That's because you grew too fast."

"All right, you two," said Mom, "that's enough of that."

Did she understand my problem? Did she care if I went around looking like some skeleton?

Damon was staring at his ice cream. "This must be walnut soup," he said in that sarcastic voice he uses sometimes.

He made me mad. "No, it's not shoop," I said, imitating his pronunciation.

Ben reached for a brownie, and Mom yanked the plate out of his reach just in time. She turned to Damon. "You stop that, Damon." She was using her hot pepper voice. Damon shut up. "And, Christy, I won't have you making fun of Damon, you hear?"

There was absolute silence except for the sound of

slurping ice cream.

I'll never forget to plug in the fridge again.

Aunt Sadie wiped her mouth and asked Mims what she wanted for Christmas. Mims sucked her finger, looked at the ceiling, and answered, "I want peace on Earth and a dollhouse."

There were giggles all around the table. "That's lovely, Mimsie," shouted Aunt Sadie. "Peace on Earth and a dollhouse. Well, honey, I do hope you get your wish."

I hoped so too. As for the dollhouse, I didn't think Aunt Sadie could afford to get that since she clerks at the variety store and isn't exactly a millionaire.

Dad was watching Mims with his spoon in the air. I had a hunch he was thinking he could make that dollhouse, and even the furniture, if only he had a new power saw. He gave a little sigh that nobody but me seemed to hear.

Mims can drive me up the wall and across the ceiling. Also, I have to admit I'm jealous of her dimples and the way the whole family hangs on her remarks. Still, I found myself wanting to buy an honest-to-gosh dollhouse for her. If I did, she'd be my slave forever. Funny what a strange feeling it gives you to have money. As somebody once said, money is power.

The trouble was that if I got the dollhouse for Mims, I ought to get Ben's tripod and Damon's strongbox and

something big for Ursula. Only I wouldn't have half enough money. And what about a new dress for me? After seeing that picture, I knew I had to have one.

It looked as if all the kids in my family wanted a big, fat share of my money, including me.

6.

What Ursula Wanted

After dinner I apologized to Damon. "I'm sorry I was mean, Damon."

"Aw, that's okay. Melted ice cream's not so bad."

"Do me a favor?"

He narrowed his eyes. "What favor?"

"Try feeling with your finger in the space where you lost your tooth."

"This some kind of joke?"

"It's not. I promise."

He stuck his finger into his mouth. "Hey, what do you know? I never even realized my new tooth's coming in." He shot me a big grin. Probably Miss Cress at church school would have called that grin a symbol of life.

46

Naturally Ben remembered to bring out the wedding pictures. While he showed them around, I slipped upstairs and into my room. I snapped on the light and stuffed a stick of gum into my mouth. I can take terrible suspense better when I'm chewing gum, and I had to find out how Priscilla Pierce tricks the crooked supermarket cashier into leaving the cereal box unguarded that contains the missing teeth, which, naturally, are actually pieces of very valuable ivory. I mean, this book really grabs your stomach and ties knots in it.

After Priscilla Pierce had succeeded in luring the cashier away from his counter and taking off with the cereal box, I put the book down and got out a pencil and piece of lined paper and made a list:

Things I Could Buy With My Money

by C. Hooper

Dollhouse for Mims
Tripod for Ben
Strongbox for Damon
Something big for Ursula (easel???)
Dress for myself

I was itching to drop in at Tucker's Store some day after school and buy a dress with no help from anybody. It was going to be green to match my eyes. There'd be long, full sleeves with matching buttons at the wrists, and a very plunging neckline. It would also have an extra wide hem so I could wear it for years, long enough so the plunging neckline would be of some use. I'd also stock up on chewing gum. If I had money left over, it would go into the bank, which should make Dad partly happy.

On the other hand, if I did that I couldn't afford the other things, and wouldn't it be selfish to keep all that money for myself, especially when Christmas was exactly one month off and I ought to be throwing myself into the spirit of unselfishness?

There was chatter in the hall downstairs, with Aunt Sadie shouting her good-byes. The front door opened and closed. From outside came the sound of a car motor barely catching, sputtering, warming up, and driving away. Aunt Sadie had left.

Now Dad would probably snatch a few quiet moments with the Sunday newspaper. I could hear Ben and Damon fooling around down there, but Dad could concentrate on his paper through a tornado.

Ursula poked her head in my door. "Chewing gum again, huh?"

"Any objections?"

"Nope. Only it makes you look like a cow, that's all."

A cow!

I let it pass. "Did Aunt Sadie like the pictures?"

"To tell you the truth, I don't think she saw them very well because she couldn't find her glasses. Damon found them after she got up. She'd been sitting on them."

"Oh, crum! Were they broken?"

"Nope. The ear pieces were bent, though. Dad straightened them with pliers. What's that you're writing?"

"It's not your business."

She shrugged. "Do me a favor and give me that perm now? I've got to have it before school tomorrow."

It certainly is hard to be alone with your thoughts and your lined paper in this house.

I slipped my list under my pillow. "What's so special about tomorrow?"

"Nothing."

"Do you want that perm, Urse?"

"You're blackmailing me."

"Right. No information, no perm. Anyway, I'll bet it's because you're giving that report for El Sharpo."

"Wellll." She was blushing. I'd hit her weak spot.

She doesn't talk much around the house about school. Usually the only way you can find out is by eavesdropping on her phone conversations. So while I was pinning her mud-colored mop into curlers, I was also trying to pin down a few facts. I mean, if she wanted me to be her slave, she ought to at least be willing to fill me in. "Listen, Ursula, what's going on?" I slammed a pin through a curler.

"Ouch! Hey, take it easy, amigo. Just because your hair's naturally curly you don't have to be so rough with mine."

"Okay, okay, but what's going on with El Sharpo? Are you and he in love with each other?"

She sighed. "He barely knows I'm living. All the other girls are in love with him too. That's why I need the easel."

"Um, sure, Ursula." With all her school expenses, I figured it would take ages for her to save up enough money from her baby-sitting. But what did an easel have to do with El Sharpo?

"So why are easels more important than tripods, Urse?"

"Did I say that?"

"Yup. After the wedding."

"Use the smaller rollers on the side, Christy."

"Okay, okay. So why are they so important?"

"Because I want tighter curls on the sides."

"I mean, why are easels so important?"

"Easels?"

"Quit stalling, Ursula. Do you want me to finish this perm, or do you want to be half curly and half straight tomorrow?" I jabbed her ear with a pin by mistake,

but all she did was tighten her lips and growl. "Well?"
I asked.

"Christy, you're the nosiest person."

"I'm not nosy. I'm merely curious."

"It's the same thing."

"So tell me why easels are important."

"All right, I'll tell you, but if you repeat it to a soul
I'll tell Ben you were the one who spilled glue on his
history book."

"That was years ago."

"So?"

"Ursula, I won't tell."

"All right. See, El Sharpo is always talking about
the European artists. He says a picture is a voiceless
poem. Isn't that beautiful?" She was staring into space.

"So?"

She gave a little jerk and came back to reality. "So
I thought I'd work up a bunch of sketches, which is
easier when you have a real easel, and sign them and
sort of casually and accidentally drop them on the floor
by his desk on my way out of class some day."

"You mean you'd go to all that trouble for that—
that person?"

"He's not 'that person.' He's a very spiritual man.
He's only teaching us Spanish while he's studying European literature in graduate school, and some day he's
going to be a famous author of poetry and essays, and

he's got deep, gorgeous eyes like two caves."

Caves? Gorgeous? Poetry and essays? Spiritual? He's probably one of those tall, skinny types with a huge Adam's apple and a voice like cotton balls.

"Christy, you're rolling that curl the wrong way."

I rolled her curl the right way, very tightly, and jabbed in a pin.

"Ouch! Christy, will you take it easy? Please!"

With her hair in those rollers she looked like a skinned poodle, and I actually felt sorry for her. It's tough to be in love when your love is unrequited. So now, to add to the confusion, I definitely knew what Ursula wanted. Which goes to show that money does not create happiness.

After I'd finished with the perm, Ursula's hair looked like a pile of wet corkscrews. How could she stand herself? "Muchas gracias," she said, and slunk away toward her room across the hall. At least she'd remembered to thank me.

All of a sudden my light went out. The entire upstairs was dark. There was only a faint glow seeping up the stairs.

Ursula screeched from across the hall. "Dad! Help!"

"What's the problem?" Dad's voice from downstairs sounded tired. But Ursula had got his attention.

"My hair dryer blew a fuse."

"All right. I'll take care of it." There was the thud-

thud of Dad's steps going down the basement stairs, and then, coming up through the register, a sort of strangled yell. "Dang blast it!"

Now what?

"The water heater's leaking." Probably the people in the next county could have heard Dad's voice.

Footsteps. Mom's footsteps, going through the kitchen toward the basement door. Mom's voice, tired and discouraged: "Can you plug it?"

Dad: I'll see.

A long pause.

Dad: I can plug it.

Mom: Thank goodness.

After a minute my light went on. So Dad had replaced the fuse. After that, a racket while he began to plug the hole in the heater.

Mom (yelling): Do you have to fix that now?

Dad (yelling): If I don't it'll cost us plenty.

Mom's footsteps going back through the kitchen toward the living room. A crash from the living room.

Mom (slightly hysterical): Ben and Damon, what's going on.

Damon: Ben knocked the chair over, and it hit the window. It was an accident, Mom.

Mom (yelling and gargling at the same time): Sure it was. But the window's just as broken.

Ben: I was demonstrating. I was showing Damon

how a boxer pivots, and I tripped.

Mom: Now you listen, Ben Hooper. You are going to put a piece of cardboard in there so we don't all freeze to death, and you are going to buy a new pane of glass, and you are going to help your father replace the old one. Hear me?

With all the jobs Dad had stacked up, he'd probably never get around to putting in more wiring.

7.

What I Did to Gilbert

Before school the next day, people crowded around to congratulate me on winning the contest. I got so excited I forgot to get rid of my gum before first-period science, and picky Mr. Casper made me go up and drop it in the wastebasket in front of the entire class.

At three o'clock, I didn't even stay for after-school volleyball. I had to get home to take a look at that check.

When I rushed in our front door, I not only got socked with the fresh smell of furniture polish but also with the envelope from WHAM sitting on the hall table with my name on it. "Pay to the order of Christine Hooper," said the check. "One hundred dollars and no cents."

I actually had it in my hand.

I still hadn't decided what to do with that check. Maybe I ought to slap it in the bank and forget about it. If I did, things would be a whole lot less messed up.

Mom called from upstairs. "That you, Christy honey?"

"Uh huh."

"Did you see the check?"

"Well, sure."

I took the check upstairs. Mom was in her room with Mims, lining the jacket of Ben's suit, making tiny stitches. The suit had big shoulders, and it was sort of a smoky gray with faint lines of blue and dark red running through it. It ought to look good with Ben's gray eyes and dark hair.

Mims was leaning against the chest that had Mom's quilt on it, sucking her finger and leafing through the picture book Aunt Sadie had given her for her birthday.

Probably Mom had all our Christmas presents made already, and wrapped and hidden. Damon and I had tried for years to find out where she keeps them, but we never had.

My mom is disgustingly efficient.

Mims looked up and smiled, making dimples big enough to drop your gum in. "Lemme see the check, Christy."

I showed it to her.

"That doesn't look like money to me."

"Nope. But I can take it to the bank, and they'll give me money for it."

"For a dumb old piece of paper?"

"Well, see—Well, they just do, that's all."

Mom snipped thread. "My daddy told me that a check is like a promise. See, it means that WHAM promises to pay that money out of what they have in the bank."

"Oh," said Mims, turning a page.

Maybe I should buy Mom a new quilting frame. She'd never suggest it, of course. She'd just wait till Dad saved up the money for the power saw so he could fix hers. Anyway, she had a whole lot of other stuff to do.

Mims was staring at a picture of a dollhouse, sucking her finger again. I knew how she felt. Sometimes you want something so much you ache.

It seemed as if everybody in our whole family wanted something so badly they'd just about kill to get it.

At dinner, Dad asked, "Did you get the check, Christy?"

"Mm-hm."

"Good. You can take it to the bank tomorrow."

"Mmm." I didn't tell him it was stashed in the bottom drawer of the bureau in Mims's and my room, underneath the red sweater I inherited from Ursula that clashes with my hair.

Dad turned to Ben. "Did you get the glass for the window?"

"Yup. And I dropped those pictures off at the Trowbridges'."

"Including the one of us?" I asked.

"Right."

"Ben, that was mean of you."

"Listen, Christy, I didn't ask you to make a face."

My fate was sealed.

On Saturday morning I sat in the kitchen reading *The Missing Teeth Mystery* while listening to Fuzz Fuller, but I didn't have any luck with the contest song. Some lady from out on Route 17 got the answer, which was "Maxie Who Drives the Taxi."

I wondered if Priscilla Pierce would have known the answer.

When Damon came to set the table for lunch, he asked, "Did you win the contest?"

"Nope. It was some song I never heard of. How's your tooth coming?"

"It's coming. It's awfully slow, though."

Sometimes life is so pokey you'd like to jab it with a pin.

The next day, Gilbert Trowbridge brought something flat to church school and showed it to Jeremy and some of the other boys. They were giggling and looking over at me while I sat there steaming.

There ought to be a Society for the Prevention of Cruelty to People.

"Gilbert," said Mr. Waterbury, running his hand over his bald spot, "will you please bring whatever you have up to me?"

When Gilbert handed the thing over, Mr. Waterbury said, "I don't see anything funny about this picture. It's a perfectly good picture, and I'm going to keep it till the end of the hour."

It was the picture of me and my family all right.

As Gilbert turned to go back to his seat, he stuck his hand in front of his mouth. A noise escaped like steam coming out of a kettle. He was smothering laughter.

After church school, everybody crowded around Mr. Waterbury's table to get their fill of the photograph. Even some of the girls started laughing, and Gilbert seemed to enjoy the fuss. He let them all have a good look before he took the thing back. I tried to act calm and unmoved, while slowly chewing my gum, but if somebody had pulled my cork, I'd have fizzed all over the room.

Out in the hall, I snuck up behind Gilbert and snatched the picture out of his hand. I tore it up into little pieces and dropped them on his head. Then I took off down

the hall while he shouted, "All right for you, Hooper, you're going to pay for that."

Gilbert's mother called Ben that afternoon and demanded another photograph. You could hear her voice all over the house. Naturally Ben was furious with me. "All right, Christy-Wisty, what got into you?"

"You should ask me what got into Gilbert. He deliberately brought that picture to church school so he could show it around for everybody to laugh at. It's so, Ben. Honestly."

"Okay, okay, I believe you. There's no other reason he'd bring it."

"You ought to charge Mrs. Trowbridge for the new one."

"Couldn't get away with that. Good will and all that kind of thing. I know it was nasty of him, but try to restrain yourself next time, huh?"

It wasn't going to be easy.

8.

What I Wanted

That evening, while Aunt Sadie was still around, I took off again to change one item on my list and add two. Now it looked like this:

Things I Could Buy With My Money

By C. Hooper

Dollhouse for Mims
Tripod for Ben
Strongbox for Damon
Easel for Ursula
Dress for myself
Quilting frame for Mom
Put check in bank for Dad

Putting the check in the bank wasn't actually buying a gift for Dad, but it might make him feel better. I'd been saving little bits of my birthday and Christmas gifts from Aunt Sadie for years, maybe a dollar each time, but even now the money in my savings account was only a few dollars. What if I changed my mind and decided to go to college after all?

Dad says education makes a person a person, but he never went to college, and he's a perfectly good person. Still, maybe he knows something I don't. So in a way my saving the money would be a gift for him, except it isn't the kind of thing you wrap in a package and tie with Mom's leftover yarn.

I closed my eyes and thought of my imaginary green dress. It would have a satiny belt, and maybe a bow in front. When I wore it to church school, the girls would be jealous, and the boys would swoon.

What would Priscilla Pierce do if she had a hundred dollars? She never seems to have trouble making up her mind, even when the bad guy is staring her in the face.

I picked up *The Missing Teeth Mystery*. Maybe it would give me moral support.

Not long after Aunt Sadie left, there was a knock on my door.

"Come in."

It was Dad with weather stripping for the window.

"You been reading this whole time, Christy?"

"Nope. I've been making out my Christmas idea list."

"Good. Time to get started making things, huh?"

"Yeah, sure."

He squinted at me. "You are going to make things, aren't you? You're not going to—"

"Well, everybody seems to need something big this year."

"They haven't been asking you for things, have they? I know Ben did, but nobody else did, I hope."

I wasn't going to squeal. "Um, see, I just sort of overheard things. Damon needs a strongbox, and Ursula needs an easel. And there's Mims and her dollhouse. I mean, they really need things, Dad."

He laid the stripping along the windowsill and pressed hard. "They do not. They can get along without them. Christy, did you put your check in the bank?"

"Um, no."

He looked me in the eye. "I can't make you do it. It's your money. But I wish you would."

I didn't know what to say.

"Think about it, will you, honeybun?"

I nodded.

He turned back to the window. "Christy, how come you never stick around when Aunt Sadie's here?"

"Aunt Sadie doesn't care. She's always talking anyway. You know you call her the town crier behind her back."

"Only in fun. She never repeats anything she shouldn't. Besides, I miss you when you go upstairs."

"That's different."

"Look, we've always told you that when we have company, you stick around unless you have a good reason not to. Then you explain before you leave."

"I didn't get a chance last week. Ben was showing those pictures. Oh, Dad, I looked so awful. My dress is way too short."

He stared out of the window. "I didn't know, Christy. I thought you looked nice."

"You would. You're a man, and men don't notice when dresses aren't right."

His face split into a grin. Then he got serious. "Maybe some of us don't, but women do, don't they?"

"You mean Mom?"

"She does notice a whole lot more than you might think."

"Maybe. Except she's always so busy. Now she's working on Ben's suit, and later on she'll be finishing the quilt."

"If I ever get my new saw." He looked sad and dreamy, as if the saw were a pet that had got lost. His hands were busy pressing down weather stripping. I can hardly remember seeing them when they weren't busy, except when he reads the paper on Sundays.

He needed that saw.

After he went away, I took another look at my list. There were four things on it that Dad could make with the help of his power saw. The dollhouse, the tripod, the easel, and the part for the quilting frame.

And there sat his saw in the garage, busted.

9.

What Gilbert Did for Me

All that week I kept exercising my brain, but by Saturday morning I wasn't any closer to making up my mind than I'd ever been. Priscilla Pierce hadn't helped. She'd been too busy recovering the missing teeth. Mims always wonders why books have to end just when everyone gets happy. Well, Priscilla Pierce may have been happy, but I wasn't.

Christmas was two weeks and three days off. Yesterday Mom had decorated the living room with candles and greens Ben had pruned from our evergreens. There was a crèche on the bookcase that used to be Mom's grandmother's.

With Christmas so close, something ought to be done. I had to quit stalling and get myself in motion.

After breakfast, while Mims was clearing the table,

Fuzz Fuller was playing the tail end of "I Love You 'Cause Your Toes Turn In." The contest song came on, and it must have been something out of ancient Greece. I mean, it meant absolute zero to me, so I guess my hundred dollars was all I was going to pry out of WHAM.

I ducked up to our room and slipped the check out of my drawer and picked up Priscilla Pierce to return to the library. As I passed Mom's room on my way back down the hall, I called out, "I'm going to the library." I took off down the stairs so she wouldn't ask questions, and I grabbed my hat and jacket.

At the library, I returned *The Missing Teeth Mystery.* I checked out *The Case of the Hollow Hobbyhorse* in paperback, stuffed it into my pocket, and headed for the bank. As Marva York, the teller who solos at our church, was cashing my check, she said, "My goodness, Christy, that's an awful lot of cash for a young girl."

"Right."

Everyone says Marva York has a beautiful contralto voice, and I wish she'd stick to her singing.

I was definitely going to do something with that money soon.

So what was I going to do?

Outside the bank, I found myself heading east inside the ridge of snow along the edge of the sidewalk. I speeded up past the variety store so Aunt Sadie wouldn't see me and ask questions tomorrow, and I hurried past Hillyer's Hardware. The junk in Hillyer's window didn't look one bit exciting. I've never been able to understand why Dad's so attracted to screwdrivers and power tools. I've been there with him a few times, and he acts like a kid in a toy store.

I kept moving, and pretty soon there I was in front of Tucker's Store, with my breath smearing up the glass of the windows. Those windows were decorated with gold and silver balls and sparkling stars. One window had games and toys, including all kinds of dolls, and another had slacks and shirts and mittens. There were dresses, all in grown-up sizes, including a long, glittery one. I wished Mom had a place to wear a dress like that, and that I had a million dollars to outfit the whole family.

I ducked inside and wandered over to the girls' clothing department. All of a sudden I felt strange and bashful. When the gray-haired saleslady smiled at me, I looked away. There was a rack of dresses that looked about my size, and I drifted toward it. "May I help you?" asked the saleslady.

"No, thank you. I'm just looking."

I flipped through the dresses. I could feel the saleslady watching from behind. There were yellow, blue, lavender, and red dresses, and dresses the color of cinnamon. There was one green dress, very dark, with short sleeves and a high neck.

I slunk away, and out through the big glass doors.

My feet led me back along the sidewalk toward Hillyer's Hardware. An invisible something pulled me inside. It wouldn't hurt to just ask Mr. Hillyer the price of a power saw. He probably wouldn't laugh at me.

I spotted two white heads toward the back of the store. One was Mr. Hillyer's. The other one belonged to a tiny woman with a pointed chin. It was Miss Cress, Damon's church school teacher.

Mr. Hillyer saw me through the top parts of his glasses. "Hi there, Christy. How's the family?"

"Fine, Mr. Hillyer."

"You all ready for Christmas?"

"Not exactly. That's why I'm here."

"Well, I'll be with you in a few minutes."

While I was waiting, I looked around. There were washers and nails and screws and staples and tacks and glazier's points and fuses and hinges and sandpaper and glue. Thank goodness somebody was interested in this kind of thing, because if nobody was, the whole country would be at a standstill, especially our house.

Miss Cress walked out with a box the size of my fist that was labeled NAILS. What was she going to do with them all? "Hello, Christy dear." She gave me a nod and a smile, and I smiled back.

"Mr. Hillyer," I asked, "are power saws expensive?"

He rubbed his chin. "Yes. But you don't have any use for one, do you?"

"No. But see, our whole house is messed up because Dad's is busted. Mom can't make her quilt and Mims won't get her dollhouse for Christmas and Ben won't get his tripod and Ursula won't get her easel, all on account of Dad's busted saw, and I won a hundred dollars in the WHAM contest by singing 'Kitty McQuitty.'" I paused for breath.

"Well! I do believe I heard something about your winning that contest. But, Christy, I wonder if you should spend so much."

"Could I get one for under a hundred dollars?"

What a dumb question! Now he was going to tell me the worst.

"What kind of power saw?" he asked.

"What kind?"

"A circular saw with a round blade?"

"Yeah, that's it, Mr. Hillyer."

"Sure you can."

Good glory!

"I can? Then I want to, Mr. Hillyer. I really do."

All of a sudden I was sure. I felt terrific, all clean and fresh, as if I'd just climbed out of Mom's washer.

"All right, Christy. But remember, you can always bring it back if you change your mind."

"I won't, Mr. Hillyer."

"What horsepower?"

What horsepower? How should I know?

I must have looked puzzled, because Mr. Hillyer scratched his head and took a look at the ceiling. "Well now, I think I might remember which one he got before. Yup. It was the most powerful one I carry, because he wanted to be able to do all kinds of things."

Dad would want to be able to do everything.

"It's mighty heavy, though. Maybe your dad could come get it."

"I'll carry it."

He wrapped it very carefully in thick paper.

It was heavy all right. When I picked it up there was this terrible strain, as if I were having all my teeth yanked out. I might never make it home with this thing. But I tightened my jaw and tried to look brave while I carried it out of the store, with Mr. Hillyer watching me and shaking his head.

As I walked past the variety store, my arms were already two enormous aches. Inside, Aunt Sadie had her back to me, ringing up a sale for a customer I couldn't see.

Smash! All of a sudden I was sprawled all over the sidewalk. Dots were chasing each other in front of my eyes.

"Hey, Hooper," called a voice, "you okay?"

It was Gilbert.

I wanted extremely much to shrivel up and blow away.

I managed to turn myself onto my side and gradually sit up. There was Gilbert all right, carrying a small paper bag from the variety store. "You skinned your knee," he said. "You must have hit that patch of ice." At least he wasn't laughing. In fact, he actually knelt and grabbed my arm and helped me up.

The saw. What had happened to the saw? I had a foggy memory of hanging onto it with both hands the whole time I was falling. Now the package sat on the sidewalk. The paper was slightly torn, but not badly. The saw must be okay.

Gilbert stuck his bag in the pocket of his jeans, leaned over, and started to pick up my package. "Hey, what you got in here, a bowling ball?" Very gradually he hoisted it up, staggering the least bit.

"It's, um, something Dad needs to make Christmas presents with."

I didn't say I'd paid for it. He might not understand how it is at our place, with five children and everybody always having to save up for things.

He looked around, probably to make sure none of his friends saw him with a girl. "You okay?" he asked again.

I bent my arms and legs, one at a time. They were

a little stiff, but they were operating. There was a tear in the right leg of my jeans. My knee, underneath, was scraped and bleeding. Gilbert dug into his pocket. He hauled out a mussed tissue and handed it to me, and I dabbed the bloody spot. "Thanks," I said.

"I'll carry this, um, thing for you," he said.

I must have wax in my ears. I couldn't believe what he'd said. He even lives in the other direction. I took a careful look at him, but he hadn't even cracked a smile. I mean, if he'd been wearing armor he could have been one of King Arthur's knights. One of the shorter ones.

As we headed toward my house, I asked, just to make sure I wasn't dreaming, "Are you kidding, Gilbert?"

"I wouldn't kid you."

"Ha! You're always saying nasty things to me. You even made fun of that picture."

"Yeah. Only I defended you afterward when Wick said you looked like a weed that got pulled up by the roots."

"That's mean. That's just plain nasty."

"That's what I told him. I said you looked more like a starving chicken."

"All right for you, Gilbert Trowbridge."

"Listen, Hooper, I didn't really say that. I was only kidding, honestly. I can't help teasing you, because you always get so stirred up."

He was smiling. And he was actually looking at me, full force. So right there on the curb, waiting for the Hercules Farm Machinery truck to pass, spraying slush onto our ankles, I smiled down at him.

I'd intended to stop for chewing gum, and to put the rest of the money in the bank, but I changed my mind. I could do that on Monday.

By the time we got to my house, Gilbert was puffing hard from the weight of the saw, and I felt kind of sorry for him. It was the least I could do. "Thanks, Gilbert. I really appreciate what you did. Would you like to come in for some hot chocolate?"

"No, thanks. It's almost lunchtime, and I've got to get home. See you tomorrow." He dumped the saw into my arms, and while I struggled up the steps with it, he took off. It wasn't all that close to lunchtime, so I guess he didn't want my family seeing us together.

Boys are stranger than anybody.

10.

I'd Rather Do It My Way

"Boys are stranger than anybody," I told Mom, who was in the kitchen arranging greens for a wedding.

"You're probably right, but exactly what are you talking about?"

"Gilbert. He's hot and cold. He's nasty to me at church school, but he carried my package home for me, right up to the front steps."

"That's nice."

"You mean it's nice about the package or about being nasty at church school?"

"You know I mean it's nice he carried the package."

"So how come he did it?"

"Because he likes you."

79

"How could he? He's always mean to me in front of his friends."

"That's because he doesn't want his friends to know he likes you. He wants to throw them off the track. Boys are like that. My mama explained that to me, because your dad was that way at Gilbert's age."

I couldn't imagine my dad being like that. In fact, I couldn't imagine his being ten years old.

"Gilbert will change," said Mom, clipping stems. "Give him two or three years."

Two or three years is an awfully long time. In two or three years his eyes could turn orange, or he could become a drug freak, or even move to another town.

Mom looked at me. "Your jeans are torn."

"I had a fall and scraped my knee."

"I'm sorry, honey. You scoot upstairs to the bathroom and wash it good and plenty, with soap and water."

I'd already stashed the saw in the closet of my bedroom, where Mims was busy pretending to read *Jack and the Beanstalk* to her dolls. Now I whizzed back upstairs and through the hall past Ursula's room, where she was painting at her desk. She was using the top of her paint box as an easel, and there were brushes and squished tubes of paint all over the place.

In the bathroom, I peeked through the hole in my jeans to examine my knee, which had turned a nauseating shade of purple. I soaped it, rinsed it, and dried it. My jeans got wet, but I didn't care.

Mims was still in the bedroom. "Fee, fi, fo, fum," she was saying. She looked up. "Your jeans are torn."

"I know."

"They're wet, too,"

"Right. Hey, Mimsy, do me a favor?"

"No. I'm in the middle of a very important story."

"Tell you what. I'll read it for you if you'll go and snitch one of those Sunday comic sections Mom saves in the storage space off her room, and some of her leftover red yarn."

"How come?"

"Because if Mom catches me she'll skin me alive. You know she doesn't like us in there, but you can get away with it because you're the youngest."

"Wellll."

"See, I got a new power saw for Dad, and I'm going to wrap it and give it to him as an early Christmas gift."

She stared at me with those puppy eyes of hers. "You mean you went and bought one?"

"Yup. I figured he could get started making gifts, like maybe dollhouses and stuff."

She nodded.

"But don't you dare tell till after I give it to him. I want it to be a surprise."

I knew that would make her feel important. Sure enough, she disappeared in the direction of Mom's room.

I never could understand why that storage space is off limits. There's only an old footlocker in there, plus a lot of odds and ends.

I picked up the book and read in a loud voice:

> "Fee, fi, fo, fum,
> I smell the blood of an Englishman!
> Be he alive or be he dead,
> I'll grind his bones to make my bread!"

Some bloodthirsty giant!

By the time Dad came home I'd wrapped the gift and patched my jeans. I cornered him in the downstairs hall and held out the package, with the Peanuts comic page on the outside and the red yarn tied in a bow. "Merry Christmas!"

He raised his left eyebrow. "Honeybun, you're a little early."

"I know. This is an early gift. Open it, Dad, would you please, before I drop it?"

"If you say so. Say, what have you got in here, rocks?" He lugged it into the living room, and we sat on the sofa while he ripped off the paper. When he saw what it was, he didn't speak. He just kept shaking his head. "Christy," he said at last, "you take this right

back to Chet Hillyer."

"Listen, Dad, it's what I wanted to do. You helped me win the contest, because I never would have known 'Kitty McQuitty' without you."

"That doesn't make any difference."

"And now you can make Mims's dollhouse and Ursula's easel and Ben's tripod and the part for the quilting frame."

"I won't take it, Christy."

I felt myself choking up. My voice came out in a sort of screech. "You've got no right to tell me what to do. Can't you see I'd rather do it my way? Can't you see?"

He gave me a long look, as if he were inspecting me for spots. Then he laid his big hand on mine and squeezed it tight and nodded. "Okay, Christy," he said in a low, scratchy voice, "I can see."

He got up quickly and took off with the saw, pulling a tissue out of his pocket.

After lunch I spotted him out in back, heading for the trash can with the old saw. He took the car and came back from the lumber-and-hardware store with all sizes and shapes of wood, plus cans of paint and a lot of metal parts. He disappeared into the basement. Up through the registers came the hum of the new motor and Dad's voice singing "New York, New York" and "San Francisco" and "Chicago (That Toddling Town)." He was all over the U.S.A. Then he sang every other song he'd ever sung, including "Kitty McQuitty," and then he sang them over again.

When I went into Mom's room to return the needle and thread from patching my jeans, Mom shook her head. "I can't understand where he found the money for that saw. He must have robbed the bank."

Well, in a way he did.

11.

Christmas Eve

After school on Monday I stopped at the bank and put the rest of my cash in, which brought my account up to forty-nine dollars and fifty-seven cents. "You're getting a pretty respectable balance," said Marva York, beaming at me.

Maybe some day I'll make that trip on the *Queen Elizabeth II* after all.

Dad was working in the basement every possible minute, sometimes late into the night. The first thing he'd made was the piece for Mom's quilting frame. Then he'd started on Christmas things. So did I. I baked brownies for Ben and stuck them in the freezer. But mostly I sewed gifts out of material from Mom's scrap box. For Mims I put together a jacket for Zinnia out of some wornout flannel pajamas of Damon's. I hemmed a scarf for Damon to take the place of the one that had never been the same since it fell in the hot chocolate during his magic act. He'd have it in time for his next show. For Mom I stuck cloves into apples and tied gold-colored yarn around them for hanging sachets.

I wrote out an I.O.U. for Ursula promising to give her two more perms, and for Aunt Sadie I borrowed Mom's sewing machine and stitched a red case for her glasses out of a frazzled winter shirt of Dad's. Now she ought to be able to keep track of those glasses.

School was out on Friday, four days before Christmas. Everybody was keeping their bedroom doors closed, making and wrapping gifts, and all kinds of whisperings were going on. That evening Dad worked in the basement again. The sound of his voice singing "God Rest Ye Merry, Gentlemen" drifted into the bedroom. As I climbed into bed, I thought Mims was asleep and I could have some peace to do some thinking.

"Christy, do you think Dad will finish my dollhouse in time?"

She wasn't asleep.

I tried to be patient. "Dollhouse? How come you're so sure he's making you one?"

There was a long silence. Probably she was sucking

her finger. Maybe I shouldn't have said what I said, but I felt it was my duty to keep her in suspense. Besides, maybe he wasn't.

"Christy."

"Huh?"

"How will Santa Claus find our stockings since we don't have a fireplace?"

Right after each of us was born, Aunt Sadie gave us a stocking from the variety store. They're red and green and white, and halfway down there's a Santa Claus. Every year we tie them to the side rails of the staircase, and every year, when I see them drooping toward the floor, I get a glow all through me.

"Mims, you know Santa always finds our stockings."

"But there's no chimney for him to come down, so how does he figure out where they are?"

"Well, um, maybe he's got a list of people without chimneys, and where they hang their stockings, so he comes in their windows and finds them."

She sighed. "I hope he's careful. I wouldn't want our window to get busted again."

Me neither.

The next morning Ursula took off to meet a couple of her friends downtown. I was just coming through the hall to see how Ben was making out with lunch when I heard the kitchen door burst open, followed by the sound of wails and sniffles. It was Ursula.

"Hey," said Ben, "what's wrong, Urse?"

"He's—he's engaged."

"Who's engaged?"

"El Sharpo's engaged. We met him in the Snack Shop with some woman, and he said she was his fiancée, and she's got crooked teeth and hardly any chin."

She plopped herself down at the table with her head on her arms, brushing two spoons and a knife onto the floor. She burst into sobs.

Ben stood there chewing his lip. He reached out and touched her shoulder and said, "You'll get over it, Urse."

"Never! I never will, ever."

He shook his head. "You and your artistic temperament." He shrugged. "Okay, if that's the way you want it. But get out of my way so I can put the napkins on the table."

"Why, you cruel, unfeeling—" Ursula yanked herself up and sort of careened out of the room past me and up the stairs. Her face was all splotchy.

The next afternoon, Dad took Ben and Damon out to the tree farm to chop down a tree. If you wait till the last couple of days, you can get a good price. The one they brought home wasn't any taller than Damon, but when Dad got it into the stand and on top of the old metal footlocker Mom had covered with a sheet, it was a whole lot taller.

Ben set his camera on the coffee table so he'd be ready to take pictures the next evening.

Damon edged over to me. "Hey, Christy, what was Mom doing while we were out getting the tree?"

"How should I know?"

"You were here, weren't you?"

"Sure, but I don't shadow Mom all the time. How come you asked me that?"

"Because I finally figured out where she hides her Christmas gifts."

"Where?"

"Think I'll tell?"

"Damon, who showed you that your tooth was coming in?"

"Well, all right. I figure she sticks them in that footlocker, and then when she brings it down from the storage space to go under the tree she takes them out. Simple, huh?"

"Right."

"So next year I'll be the first one to get a look at Mom's presents."

Unless I beat him to it.

While we were decorating the tree, Dad sang "Deck the Halls" and "Joy to the World" off key, and we all

joined in, even Ursula, who seemed to be feeling better. We hung lights, and red and gold bows, and eggs in bright colors that Ursula had decorated last year. Dad lifted Mims so she could set the star at the top.

After we'd stashed gifts around the tree, Ben turned on the lights. I took a step backward and just gazed at it. Nobody was singing now. We were all absolutely silent.

Tomorrow evening Aunt Sadie would come, and we'd open our gifts and hang up our stockings before the late candlelight carol service at church. The next morning, Christmas morning, we'd take our stockings up to Mom and Dad's big bed. In the afternoon Aunt Sadie would come for the enormous dinner we'd all get ready, with turkey and mashed potatoes and cranberry sauce. Mom never holds back the food at Christmas.

After Aunt Sadie came on Christmas eve, Dad switched on the tree lights. Mom turned on the radio to Christmas music and lit the candles on either side of the crèche, making the room all shadowy and glowing, like magic.

Dad and Ben and Damon took turns playing Santa and passing out the gifts. Mims was sucking her finger. She'd been sucking it a lot lately. She must be disappointed because she'd realized there was nothing under the tree shaped like a dollhouse. I wondered too.

Ben and Damon together gave me a big box of chewing gum from the drugstore. Ursula gave me a gorgeous painting she'd done of our house, with those smudgy green bushes around it. Along the bottom she'd lettered CASA HOOPER, which, she told me, means Hooper House in Spanish. So why didn't she just call it that? Anyway, there was only one spatter on it, which could have been a bird.

Dad's gift was the frame for it, all ridged and smoothed and stained so it glowed, and Mims had made me a green change purse stitched in white. The stitches were pretty even, so Mom must have helped her. Aunt Sadie gave me a five-dollar bill.

Mom had given Damon some beanbags for juggling, and he was busy practicing with them, getting all breathless, like somebody running upstairs. "Stay away from the window, huh, Damon?" said Ben as he set up his new tripod and stuck his camera on top so it looked like a daddy longlegs. Ursula was already posing at her easel, which I imagined she'd find plenty of use for, even though El Sharpo had betrayed her.

Damon dropped the beanbags and grabbed his new strongbox, which Dad had made of wood, with metal hinges and a padlock, and was a whole lot better looking than an ordinary metal one.

I grabbed Ursula's water color, and Ben set the delayed-action button on his camera. "Everybody say cheese."

We gathered together for the flash, huddling close.

There were still a few presents around the footlocker. Ben came at me with an enormous package wrapped in comics and tied with green yarn. This had to be from Mom.

Sure enough, the card said,

> *Christmas Love to Christy*
> *From Mom*

Inside the paper there was something soft and green.

A green dress, to match my eyes.

For me. Personally.

The neckline was round. It wasn't very low, but it was okay. The sleeves were full, and wrist length. The skirt was much the longest I'd ever owned, with a very wide hem. In this dress, I was sure to make Gilbert go soggy in the knees. "Oh, Mom!" I was in her arms, hugging her and getting hugged, feeling her cheek against mine.

Maybe I should have guessed, but how could I when I'd never had a dress of my own? Mom must have made it ages ago. No wonder she didn't want me poking around the storage space.

Now there was the sound of Dad's steps stamping up from the basement. He showed up in the living-room doorway holding something big and square. It was Mims's dollhouse. Gray, with dark green shutters. Exactly like our house. A perfect copy.

Dad set it on the floor and rubbed his hands. "The paint finally got dry," he said. "Thought it never would."

Mims had taken her finger out of her mouth and was staring. All of a sudden she let out a shriek, flew across the room, and hugged the house. "It's beautiful," she hollered. "It's so beautiful!"

There'd be plenty of furniture for it before long. I guess my dad is about the handiest man in town.

He knelt and kissed Mims. "Listen, everybody, I want to make sure you all know who's responsible for nearly all my gifts to you." He gave me a bow. "It's Miss Christine Hooper. By spending her contest money for my saw, she's given us a big chunk of our Christmas."

"Terrific!" said Damon.

"Hey, hey!" said Ben.

"Not bad," said Ursula, who actually smiled.

Mom beamed at me.

In fact, everyone was beaming at me except Mims, who was busy poking her nose inside the dollhouse.

12.

Christmas Morning

Naturally I wore my new dress for the carol service. It wasn't a bit bad on me. Oh, maybe my neck seemed the least bit scrawny, and there was a scab on my knee that looked like a smashed strawberry, but mostly I was satisfied.

Ben's new suit set off his gray eyes and that square chin of his so he looked almost grown up. Damon seemed human now that he had his entire new tooth. He had on clean pants and a checked shirt you could have eaten your dinner off of. Mims was all pink, like peppermint stick ice cream, and Ursula's perm had calmed down so it didn't look as if she'd been struck by lightning.

"Everybody ready?" asked Dad, pulling gloves onto

those big hands of his.

"Christy, get that gum out of your mouth this minute," said Mom, shaking her head so her curls jumped.

Maybe that's why I chew gum. It's a great way to get attention.

Inside the vestibule of the church, we were taking off our coats when I noticed Ursula smiling at Rich Philby, who's also in eighth grade. He's got little dark eyes and fat cheeks and crooked teeth, but they didn't keep him from grinning back. I mean, Rich Philby! I will never understand eighth graders.

Gilbert walked in with his family. His hair was all slicked down except for that one lock that points toward the ceiling like some antenna. He edged up to me. "Hey, Hooper," he mumbled into my ear, "you look okay."

"Thanks, Gilbert."

"Only your knee looks like raw hamburger."

I would have hauled off and socked him right there in the church vestibule if he hadn't been shooting me an enormous, gorgeous grin that definitely meant more than friendship.

Mims always falls asleep with Dad's arm around her during the carol service. I always get goose bumps, which hit me hardest at the end when the church goes dark and the choir members light candles and sort of float down into the aisles and we all sing "Silent Night" and the chimes strike twelve and suddenly it's Christmas. This time it wasn't any different.

Mims's voice woke me up, calling from our doorway across to Dad and Mom's room. "Pleeese can't we go down now and bring our stockings up?"

It was Christmas morning.

"All right, Mims," Mom answered. "Wake everyone up, and tell them to hustle."

"I'm awake," called Damon. "I've been awake for hours, but Ben won't get up. He keeps telling me to shut up."

I struggled into my scuffies and robe and followed Damon and Mims and Ursula downstairs. Ben thumped along behind me, with a yawn that sounded like air being let out of a balloon.

All five stockings were crammed full, each one with a gingerbread man poking his head out. Ursula untied Mims's stocking for her. Ben grabbed his in one hand and his tripod and camera in the other. Damon took a bite out of his gingerbread man, even though we're supposed to wait till we get up to Dad and Mom's bed. I guess he was in a hurry to try out his new tooth.

By the time I made it back upstairs, Mims was snuggled under the covers between Dad and Mom. And there it was on top of them. The quilt.

Red, blue, green, lavender, and yellow stars were sprinkled all over it, like flowers in the snow.

So naturally I had to crawl in beside Dad. I guess I took over more than my share of the quilt, but I felt entitled to it.

Damon scrambled in next, and then came Ursula. "Say cheese, everybody," said Ben. He set his camera for the delayed-action photo, and then he dove in with us.

Just before the camera clicked, I remembered to smile.

Travel back in time to 1914!

ALL-OF-A-KIND FAMILY
by Sydney Taylor

Meet a *very* special family living on New York's Lower East Side. There's Mama, Papa, five daughters, and a son. Rich in kindness though poor in money, they live amid immigrants, pushcarts, horse-drawn carriages, and stoves heated by coal. It's a time when girls wear high-buttoned shoes, boys wear knickers—and soda cost a penny. Truly wonderful, heartwarming stories you'll love about a very close, old-fashioned Jewish family!

☐ ALL-OF-A-KIND FAMILY 40059-7-75 $2.95
☐ ALL-OF-A-KIND FAMILY DOWNTOWN 42032-6-57   2.75
☐ ALL-OF-A-KIND FAMILY UPTOWN 40091-0-59   1.95